Pinch Me

Pinch Me

Gabrielle Prendergast

orca soundings

ORCA BOOK PUBLISHERS

Library and Archives Canada Cataloguing in Publication

Prendergast, Gabrielle, author
Pinch me / Gabrielle Prendergast.
(Orca soundings)

Issued in print and electronic formats.
ISBN 978-1-4598-1364-9 (paperback).—ISBN 978-1-4598-1365-6 (pdf).—
ISBN 978-1-4598-1366-3 (epub)

I. Title. II. Series: Orca soundings
PS8631.R448P55 2017   jc813'.6   c2016-904464-5
c2016-904465-3

First published in the United States, 2017
Library of Congress Control Number: 2016950098

Summary: In this high-interest novel for teen readers, pop sensation
Darius Zaire wakes up to discover he has somehow been transported
back to his old, completely ordinary life.

*Orca Book Publishers is dedicated to preserving the environment and has
printed this book on Forest Stewardship Council® certified paper.*

Orca Book Publishers gratefully acknowledges the support for its
publishing programs provided by the following agencies: the Government
of Canada through the Canada Book Fund and the Canada Council
for the Arts, and the Province of British Columbia through
the BC Arts Council and the Book Publishing Tax Credit.

Cover image by iStock.com

ORCA BOOK PUBLISHERS
www.orcabook.com

Printed and bound in Canada.

20 19 18 17 • 4 3 2 1

For Bronwen and Calum

Chapter One

I tripped over a girl at the top the of the stairs. Landing with a dull thump, I was grateful for the expensive shag carpet. This was the fourth semiconscious girl I'd seen since I left the stragglers of the party in the pool house. The girl giggled a little and curled into a ball under the side table. Her miniskirt rode up at the back, and I could see her pink panties.

They were the color of a fruity cocktail and made me feel a bit nauseous.

Maybe that last daiquiri was a bad idea.

"Billy?" I called out. He had to be up there. Probably in my office. *My* office. That was a laugh. The only person to do officey type stuff in there was Billy—my manager. Right now he wasn't managing very well. My Bel Air mansion was full of drunk and/or unconscious groupies. Both male and female. And at least a few who seemed to be a bit of both. It was Billy's idea to have a party after the Teen Picks Awards show I'd hosted. Now he could get these leeches out of here.

"BILLY?!"

Mercifully, someone downstairs turned off the music. Finally. There were only so many times I could listen to my own songs.

I heard Billy's voice coming from my office.

"It's a great facility," he said in a cheerful voice. "You'll like it much better than the other places."

A gruff rumble was the only reply. I pushed the door open.

Billy was leaning on the desk. My dad was slumped in a chair in front of him.

"Darius!" Billy said. "I thought you'd gone to bed."

I rubbed my face. I was wiped out. I knew I *should* go to bed. But I didn't trust Billy not to bail on me and leave all these strangers in my house.

"Can you clear everyone out?" I asked. It came out pretty slurred, but Billy got the idea.

"Sure thing, Darius. Hey, great news! Your dad has agreed to go to rehab."

"Again?"

Dad just mumbled from the chair. He was obviously wasted.

"Where to this time?" I asked. "And how much is it going to cost me?"

"Don't worry. It's affordable," Billy said.

That didn't mean much. I was a multimillionaire teen R & B sensation. One of the richest teens on earth. Rehab on the space station would have been affordable to me.

"Whatever," I said. This would be the third time in two years I'd paid for my dad to go to rehab. It was getting a little old. "As long as you arrange everything. And kick all these losers out of my house."

I stumbled out of there, trying to wipe the image of my old drunk dad out of my mind. I wondered how long he'd last in rehab this time. Two weeks was his record. Maybe he'd beat it.

My bedroom was downstairs. But I didn't think I'd make it back there without falling over again. So I decided to sleep in the video-games room. I pushed the door open and fell onto the big leather couch. Lucky for me, it was unoccupied. That would have been awkward.

The room spun around me as I wriggled out of my jeans. I was grateful for the leather couch. At least if I barfed it would be easy to clean up. My cleaning lady, Gloria, already thought I was a degenerate. I doubted I could have sunk any lower in her eyes.

I rolled over and focused on the dim ceiling in hopes that the room would stop spinning. It didn't really help, but it gave me time to think. Not that I really wanted to. My life was a mess. The awards show had gone okay, and my latest album was selling well. But everything else was a disaster. I'd been matched in the tabloids with another starlet—Jo-Dee Justice— whose synth-pop music made my stuff sound like Mozart.

To make things worse, Billy thought I should take Jo-Dee Justice out in public. He was worried about the rumors that I was gay. As if it mattered. Actually, it turned out *she* was gay. She swore me to secrecy on our first "date." She begged me to help her career by pretending we were together. I didn't want to make a scene in the fancy restaurant, so I agreed.

Suddenly I had a lesbian girlfriend. Yay me.

The problem was, she kept other girls away. And I kind of wanted a real girlfriend. For the past four years girls had been throwing themselves at me. I indulged once in a while. Who wouldn't? But it was never very long before they wanted money and cars and "help with their careers." That was getting pretty old too.

I was getting old. I was nearly eighteen and already bored with life. It had been four years since a cheesy love-song video I'd made in my backyard had gone viral and turned me into an R & B superstar. Since then it felt like I'd been everywhere and done everything. I'd grown up on the red carpet and TV talk shows. I fell out of limos in front of the top nightclubs. I survived multiple disgusting or bizarre rumors. And I spent money on people because I had nothing better to do.

At least when I spent it on people I cared about, I enjoyed it. Mom, mainly. I bought her a car and a nice apartment in downtown Vancouver. I had tried to get her to come live with me in Los Angeles, but she was hesitant to leave her job. Her elderly clients needed her. She was devoted to them.

My dad crawled out of the woodwork pretty soon after I got famous. He said he wanted to keep an eye on me. It seemed like a good idea. He'd been in the music biz when he was younger, so he knew what to expect.

At first it was okay, because I was enjoying getting to know him. But being back in the lifestyle was too much for him. Pretty soon he started drinking again. So then I had to spend money on his rehab. I didn't enjoy that as much. When I turned eighteen, I knew I could just kick his sorry white ass to the curb. But I wasn't sure I was that brave.

Damn, I wished the room would stop spinning.

The door opened a crack, letting the light from the hallway in.

"Darius…" a high voice said. A girl. Drunk. Billy made sure all the girls at the party were over twenty-one. He didn't want any trouble about underage drinking. But from what I could tell, most of them were more like thirty. And they were slobbering all over me, which was pretty gross. Everybody wanted a piece of Darius Zaire.

"Hi, Darius…"

She stood at the end of the couch, outlined by the light behind her. A skinny white girl. Teetering on giant high heels, in a dress that barely covered her boobs. I sighed.

"Hi...did I get your name?"

"Dixee. It's spelt with two *e*'s."

"Why not three?" I said.

She giggled and climbed on top of me.

"Uh...I was just going to go to sleep."

"That's fine," she said, squeezing in beside me. "We can just cuddle."

I didn't have the energy to argue. And since I was a little worried I'd barf in my sleep, I figured it was probably safer to have company. I closed my eyes.

Her hand inched up my thigh, toward the leg of my Ralph Lauren boxers.

"Moxie..."

"Dixee," she corrected.

"Right, Dixee. I really just want to sleep."

She moved her hand away. I lay there listening to her breathing. I tried not to think. Sleep was finally creeping up on me.

"Are you really falling asleep?" Dixee asked. I heard her, but it was like she was far away. I was drifting into la-la land. "Hey, asshole, wake up!"

I felt her shove me. Hard. Then I felt my body being ejected from the couch. I expected the floor to come up to meet me—painfully. But I just kept falling.

Chapter Two

BANG!

The floor was *hard*. My cheek slammed down on something sharp. I rolled onto my face.

"Crap. Why did…?" Ugh, my mouth was filled with grit. I was going to have to talk to Gloria about the state of this floor. It was disgusting. I scraped the crud out of my mouth. I was ready to kick the girl out. Pushing me off my own couch? No more Mr. Nice Guy. I needed to stop being such a doormat.

My hand felt around for the sharp thing I had landed on. It was a piece of LEGO. Weird. I hadn't owned LEGO in years. I wiped my face again and sat up.

Wow. I must have been drunker than I thought. The room looked all gray and messed up. From the light I could tell the sun was coming up, but...

"Hey, Pixie, what time is it?" I turned to look at the girl.

There was no girl there. No leather couch either.

"What the...?"

No big-screen TV. No giant Banksy-style mural on the wall. No Noguchi coffee table.

"DARREN!"

Was that my mom's voice? What was she doing here? I jumped to my feet, planning to try to clean up a bit.

I didn't want my mom to see the mess of the previous night's party. I looked around, my eyes adjusting to the low light. I didn't understand what I was seeing.

It was nothing but an ordinary teenager's bedroom. A bit more squalid than some, maybe. But ordinary. The worst part of it was that I recognized it. It was *my* old bedroom. The one in mom's old townhouse on Boundary Road. The townhouse she had rented before I bought her the condo in Coal Harbour.

"What the hell is going on?" I said to my empty room.

"DARREN!" My mom's voice echoed through the open door. She was calling up the stairs. "Get your butt down here! You're going to be late!"

She called me *Darren*. She hadn't called me Darren for a couple of years, after I'd finally convinced her to call me Darius.

I stood up and yelled down the stairs, "Mom, I—" Holy crap. Those stairs looked like they could collapse at any moment. "I don't feel well!"

"Darren David Zegers, don't you give me that nonsense!" she yelled back. "You were singing in the shower last night like Marvin Gaye on steroids. Get dressed and get down here!"

I ducked back into my room. What a mess. I had forgotten what a slob I used to be. *Used to be!* Was this some kind of time-travel thing? Maybe that was it. Was I back to being a fourteen-year-old nobody?

I stepped over to the mirror. And swore. Loud.

"Young man, I heard that! You watch your mouth!"

I wasn't fourteen. I was tall and had whiskers. I lifted up my T-shirt. Yep. A few hairs on my chest. I tried my voice out.

"Hello," I said to the mirror. "My name is Darius Zaire." Deep. Still a tenor, but definitely a man's voice. And my hair was shorter than I remembered. Had I had a haircut and forgotten? That seemed like something I would do. And where did I get these tragic boxer shorts?

"Mom! What's the date today?"

She told me the date, in between a few other choice words. So I *was* almost eighteen. But I wasn't where I was supposed to be. What was going on?

I grabbed the first clothes I could find. A cheap pair of track pants and a radio-station T-shirt. I found some faded sneakers too. After rinsing out my furry mouth in the bathroom, I chewed up two painkillers to deal with the crushing headache that was blooming in my skull. Then I raced down the wobbly stairs.

Mom was standing in the kitchen, looking irritated. Her hair looked weird.

For years I'd been paying for her to get it braided at an expensive salon. But it looked like it used to—tugged back into a boring bun with a halo of frizz. And her clothes weren't the nice boutique stuff I'd sent her from LA. They were Walmart dull.

This was getting real. Had I forgotten a trip to Vancouver to visit Mom? Had Billy been pocketing the money I sent her?

"We ran out of bread, so you'll have to buy lunch." She handed me five bucks. "I'm doing a diabetes-management workshop in Surrey today that goes to nine, so I won't be home until late. You can fix noodles for dinner, right?"

I stood there. Dumb as a post.

"Noodles, Darren? Can you do it?"

"Yes," I lied. "Hey, Mom, why don't you live in the Coal Harbour condo anymore?"

"What Coal Harbour condo?"

"The one I bought you."

She stared at me for a second before bursting into laughter. "With your lawn-mowing money? You're too funny." She handed me a backpack I didn't recognize. "Band is canceled today, so you don't need your sax. Oh, and why don't you drop into Garden City on the way home? I heard they were looking for part-timers."

"I have a job already," I said.

"Oh, really? And what is that?"

The game was getting annoying. Maybe it was some joke cooked up by Billy to break me out of the bad mood I'd been in. I didn't think it was very funny.

"I'm a singer, Mom. I'm Darius Zaire."

She laughed again. "Of course you are, honey. And I'm Nina Simone. Get going. The school bus will be here any minute."

"The school bus?"

"Have you hit your head, son? The school bus that takes you to the only school that knows what to do with you. Hurry down to the corner."

I couldn't think of anything to do but go along with it. Maybe there would be some hilarious surprise party at the end of it. I wasn't really in the mood for another party, but what choice did I have? I grabbed the hoodie Mom handed me and headed out the door.

"Darren," she said.

I turned back.

"Haven't you forgotten something?"

I was stumped. I had my backpack, a hoodie, money for lunch. What else did a kid need for school?

"Where's my hug, son?"

I walked back and put my arms around her. And squeezed. She patted my back a few times.

"Have a good day, honey," she said.

I didn't want the hug to end. I knew I was in the wrong place or the wrong time. Or that something, somehow, was terribly wrong. But that hug made me feel better than I'd felt in months. Maybe years. I almost felt like I was going to cry. I cleared my throat to cover it.

"I'll miss the bus, Mom," I said before kissing her on the cheek.

Then I ran for the corner and got there just as the yellow bus pulled up.

Chapter Three

The school bus was about as bad as I expected it to be. Cracked vinyl seats. Something rattling in the engine. Vague smell of death. It occurred to me as I got on and sat down that I didn't even know what school I went to. Last time I remembered going to school, it was to one four blocks from the townhouse.

Why was I taking the bus? Then I had a horrible thought.

Before the video had gone viral and I was offered that TV show in Toronto, Mom had been trying to get me into a special program at a school on the other side of town. A program for losers like me who could barely read. When I started the show, I had a tutor on set. She gave me pointless worksheets and helped me learn my lines. I had a great memory, so that was easy. Then the album topped the charts, and I went on tour. The tutor came with me. As soon as I was old enough to quit school altogether, I did. So why was I going to school now?

This was some kind of nightmare. That's it, I thought. I'm having a nightmare on the floor of my video-game room. That skinny white girl, Taxi or whatever, is snoring on the couch.

Billy is clearing out my house. In the morning Gloria will come and mop up all the stains. I'll wake up to a nice clean mansion. Just me and my saxophone and grand piano. I closed my eyes and smiled at that thought.

HONK!

"Get off the road, you idiot!"

The bus driver made a rude gesture out the window as a skinny white kid ran around the front of the bus. The bus stopped, and the kid got on. He looked familiar—long ratty hair and a wasted expression on his pasty face. I smiled and nodded at him.

"Hey, D," he said to me as he passed. I turned and watched him take a seat at the back of the bus. Finally I recognized him. Keir Brewster. Keir had been one of my entourage when the celebrity thing took off. He'd even come out to Toronto with me—something to do with his mom being a makeup artist.

We had been good friends for a while. But he'd gotten a little too into the party lifestyle and fallen to pieces.

I had always wondered what became of him. I guessed I finally knew. Back to normal life. Back to high school. Just like me, apparently. I glanced back to see he was lying down on the long bench. He looked like he was sleeping. That much hadn't changed.

We arrived at the school just as it started to rain. Living in LA, I had forgotten about Vancouver's incessant autumn rain. As soon as the bus door opened, I ran for the entrance. But there were a bunch of kids there, and we all had to shove through the doors. By the time I got through, my hoodie was soaked. Great way to start a day.

I had no idea where to go. Whether this was a joke or a nightmare, the deal was that I had some kind of life here. So I would have a class schedule,

I supposed. But I had no idea what it was. What was I going to do? I was considering finding the nurse's office and claiming mental breakdown when I heard my name, my *old* name, being called over the intercom.

"*Darren Zegers, please report to the office. Darren Zegers to the office, please.*"

So this will be the surprise, I thought. About time. I had things I wanted to do that day. I was working on a new song. I wanted to hit the gym. I needed shoes. You know, important stuff. This little prank would be over soon. I'd go to the office and there would be some kind of entertaining on-camera scene. Then Billy and I would fly back down to LA in a private jet and laugh our asses off about how hilarious he was.

Right. Billy was so freakin' hilarious.

I had no idea where the office was, so I wandered around a bit until I found a sign. I followed it to the office and checked in with the secretary.

"I'm Darius...I mean, Darren Zegers," I said. The secretary didn't even look up.

"Go on in," she said, waving her hand in the direction of a back office. I dragged myself in there. It had been a while since I'd been in school. But I still remembered that getting called into the office wasn't good.

"Good morning, Darren," an old bald dude said. "Take a seat." I guessed he was the principal or vice-principal. I probably should have checked the door on the way into the office. But I wasn't that quick-thinking. I sat down across from his desk. Maybe we would discuss my schedule so I could figure out where I was supposed to be.

"So, Darren, we need to talk about your grades."

Well. No such luck then.

"You're hanging in there with math and science," the bald dude said. "Acing music, of course, and drama. But these English and history grades are…"

He pushed a few papers across the desk. An essay with a big red F on it. A quiz with another F. The words swam in my vision. I had to read a comment three times before I was able to figure it out.

Your answers are too short and full of spelling mistakes. See me after class.

I guessed I hadn't bothered seeing whoever wrote that.

"I have pretty bad dyslexia," I said.

Bald dude frowned at me. "We know that, Darren. That's why you're in this program. But you should be able to pass these adapted courses."

Even though it wasn't really my life, I felt terrible. This guy I'd never met had made me feel about two inches tall. I was obviously a moron. He thought so anyway.

"What do I need history and English for anyway?" I said defensively. "I'm going to be a…" I nearly said *singer*. But I thought of how that sounded. Like a little kid who lives in a dream world. Maybe that's what had happened. Maybe I'd been living in a dream world all this time.

"A what, Darren? What are your plans for the future?"

"I don't know. Maybe something with music."

"Well, you're certainly a talented musician. But it's hard to make a good living with music."

I couldn't help it. I started to giggle. If this was a prank, it was going to be great viewing. Bald dude just looked at me.

"I don't see what's funny," he said.

He was right. I'd obviously lost my mind. And after nearly four years in the entertainment business, I had learned one thing for certain. Mental illness is no laughing matter.

Chapter Four

I arrived at my first class late. My teacher didn't look very surprised.

"Glad you could join us, Mr. Zegers," she said. Just like something out of a movie. In fact, I thought I'd done a scene just like this on that TV show I worked on four years ago. Or someone worked on. Maybe that wasn't me. Maybe there never was a TV show.

"Are you going to sit or just stand in the doorway for the whole hour?"

I sat in the first available desk I could find. It probably wasn't the desk I usually sat in, but I didn't care. At least I was in the right class. That was a miracle.

"Okay, let's take out last night's homework."

Oh no. Homework was never really my thing. As my classmates pulled out notebooks, I dug convincingly in my backpack. I didn't find anything that was obviously...what was this class anyway? I turned around to one of my classmates, a tiny kid with giant glasses. He looked like some kind of bug. But his notebook read *Redial English 4*. No. *Remedial* English. Redial English is not a thing.

I dug a bit more in my backpack. Finally I came up with a notebook. I dreaded to see what was inside it.

Leaving it closed on my desk, I tried to look as uninteresting as possible. Hopefully, the teacher, whoever she was, wouldn't call on me.

"So at the end of yesterday's class I asked you to go online and find a poem that represented something that was going on in your life. It could be a famous poem or a poem from someone's Instagram. Even song lyrics. What did everyone find?"

The kid with the big glasses shot his hand up. He read a short poem about being nobody. At least it was short. The poor kid had trouble with every word. Then I remembered that I had trouble reading out loud too. I prayed the teacher wouldn't call on me. Just out of curiosity, I opened my notebook and flipped to the last page of notes. Sure enough, there was a poem there. It was called "Stupid." And under the title it read *By Darius Zaire*.

What the…? Was Darius Zaire a different person in this bizarro world? I struggled to read through the first lines of the poem. A lot of words had been crossed out and rewritten. And even I could tell there were some spelling mistakes. I doubt I could have corrected them though.

"Darren? Would you like to share?"

I slammed my notebook shut. From what I had read of the poem, it was too embarrassing for words.

"No, miss. I don't…uh…I didn't do it." Getting detention for not doing homework was better than being humiliated in front of all these people. I closed my eyes for a second. What was going on? Since when was I too shy to talk in front of a crowd? I had just hosted the Teen Picks Awards the night before in front of thousands of screaming kids. What was a classroom of twenty?

The teacher wasn't impressed by my lie. She just crossed her arms and looked at me. I could feel my face getting red. Red faces look bad enough on white kids. On brown kids like me, they tend to make it look like you've been beaten up.

I flipped my notebook open again.

" *'Stupid,' by Darius Zaire*," I said. "Do you know who Darius Zaire is?"

"Yes, Darren," the teacher said in a bored voice. "That's the name you put on all your creative work. Thank you for writing your own poem. That's very impressive. As usual."

Wait a second. I was a good student in this class?

"Can we hear the poem?"

Here was the thing. If I had written this poem the way I write all my stuff, I would have memorized it as I wrote so I didn't have to try to read it back. Whenever I tried to read things out loud, even things I wrote myself, I screwed it up.

Got all tongue-tied. Couldn't read words. I usually just wrote lyrics in my head and got Billy or someone else to write them down.

But now I was stuck. I had to read this one, which I should have known, since I wrote it, but, of course, I'd never seen it before. Do you see my dilemma?

"Come on, Darren," the teacher said. "We don't have all day."

"*'Stupid,' by Darius Zaire*," I repeated. I looked at the scrawled words. They blurred and rearranged themselves and got all fuzzy. And I was just about to give up when I thought, what the heck. I'll just freestyle.

"*Stupid is as stupid does. That's everything I was*," I started. And then I was rapping, and then singing. That was the only thing that felt natural. I kept going with it.

And you know that it's because I can't read.

*What I need is a way to feed my mind
without being so unkind.*

*Putting words in front of me is like
cutting down a tree,*

Like a bullet in my knee,

And I think we can agree on that.

So what does my future hold?

Everything I'm told is lies,

Like there won't be a prize

*For someone with such messed-up
eyes.*

*I can't see words the way I'm
supposed to,*

*Even though I can speak and sing
and think*

As good as you and you and you.

*So what is true? A gas station?
A grocery store?*

Can't I expect more?

*Or have you already tallied up my
score*

And marked it "stupid"?

The class went quiet. I looked down at my page and realized, as the words finally became clear, that I had free-styled the exact words on the page. How did that happen?

"Wow," the teacher said. "That was wonderful work. Really wonderful. Well done, Darren."

The whole class applauded. I couldn't remember ever feeling that good at school. It wasn't exactly the Hollywood Bowl, but it would do.

My next class was a computer lab. I sat at a terminal right at the back so the lab tech wouldn't notice me googling. I needed to try to figure out what was going on. If this was a very elaborate joke put together by Billy, then surely he wouldn't be able to hack into Google and get rid of all evidence of my life.

Would he? So this was the moment I would find out if this was a joke or if I was going crazy. I wasn't sure if I was ready to know.

The lab tech came in and said something about working on "integrated studies," which sounded pretty scary. I ignored him and logged onto Google straightaway. I typed in "Darius Zaire." Then I closed my eyes, crossed my fingers and prayed. To Google. I prayed to Google. That's pathetic.

When the results came up, the first thing was not my website, or my listing on iTunes. It was something about a dude called Darius who traveled to Zaire in 1990 to work with orphaned rhinos. Then there was the Facebook page of a guy called Darius with something unpronounceable as a last name. He lived in the province of Zaire and was studying some other unpronounceable thing. Then there were three guys with names that were almost Darius Zaire but not quite.

I tried an image search. A page of dudes who weren't me, then another page of dudes with no shirts on. Quite a few pictures of Zaire, the country now referred to as the Democratic Republic of the Congo. Zebras and giraffes and stuff. Nothing about me.

Okay. That was weird. I decided to try looking up things I knew should have some mention of me. I looked up the Grammy Awards. Surely the time I won Best New Artist when I was fourteen would be listed on their site. But no. Some white rapper from Seattle was listed. Then I googled the Glastonbury Festival and looked up the page about the year I had headlined. But that year the headliner was some big-breasted English girl. The charts, I thought. My hits must be on the charts. I looked up *Billboard* magazine and went through its historical lists. Nothing. I remembered the exact date I'd hit number one with my third single. But it wasn't there. It wasn't anywhere.

Darius Zaire was gone. The only place his name appeared was on my Remedial English homework. I looked out the bright window and tried not to panic. But what was I supposed to do when I felt like I was losing my mind? Was all that stuff—the YouTube sensation, the TV show, the hit records—a dream? And if it was a dream, why couldn't I remember anything about this other life? The normal life?

I needed help. If I was going to make it through even a single day, I needed to talk to someone who might know me well enough to catch me up on myself. I dug in my backpack again and whispered a silent thanks to Mom when I came up with a fully charged phone. I didn't know who to call though.

I wasn't ready to talk to Mom about it. She would freak. And probably Billy wouldn't know who I was. Dad was obviously out. Even if he was part of this life, he was likely to be useless.

I stared at the phone, trying to remember anyone from my old life whose number I knew. The only person I could think of was Susan Koh. And I only remembered her phone number because I'd had a crush on her since I was a nobody. I'd memorized her number when I was twelve, and it still scrolled through my head sometimes. At low points usually, when I least needed reminding of what a jerk I had been to her.

But I was desperate. I typed her number into the text app. Then I texted her.

Susan. It's Darren Zegers. Maybe this is weird, but I need to see you.

It took me three tries to get *weird* close enough for even autocorrect to know what I wanted. A minute went past. I watched my phone like a creep. Finally a message popped up.

Why would it be weird? I AM your girlfriend. I'll meet you at lunch in the caf. PS. YOU'RE weird.

Wait. What?

Susan Koh was my girlfriend?

Chapter Five

The cafeteria was about as hellish as I expected. Things were flying through the air. It smelled of old fish. About five people said hi to me, forcing me to squeak back at them because I had no idea who they were. Another five gave me dirty looks. I didn't know if it was because I was some kind of loser everyone hated or some kind of bully who picked on them.

And where was I supposed to sit? School cafeterias have all kinds of rules about that, don't they? I got in line for food so I wouldn't have to decide. With the five bucks Mom gave me, I bought a muffin that looked sort of healthy, an apple and a Diet Coke. My personal trainer had told me to stop drinking sugary things. I mean the trainer I thought I had, who I'd probably imagined or something. Every decision I made was weird now. Every thought I had felt like it didn't quite fit. As I was standing with my sad little lunch, wondering where to sit, two slender arms slipped around my waist from behind. Whoever it was had nails painted green and multiple plastic bracelets. I squirmed around, and there she was.

Susan Koh. God, she was just as beautiful as I remembered. Wavy black hair, smiling eyes and a set of lips so heart-shaped they looked like something from a cartoon. She grinned up at me.

"Since when do you drink diet soda?" she asked.

"I…uh…bought it by mistake."

She took my hand and led me to a half-empty table. We sat at one end. At the other, some stoned-looking kids said something to me. I just nodded and smiled because I couldn't hear anything. My ears were ringing. Susan Koh was holding my hand. She really was my girl-friend. How on earth had I managed that?

"You look like you've had a rough morning," she said.

"You have no idea."

I started picking at my muffin, which was as stale as cardboard. But it gave me something to do with my hands.

"Want to talk about it?" Susan said.

She had always been like that. Always ready to listen to any problems

I had. Always supportive and encouraging of my crazy ideas. Since fifth grade, when we met, she had been the person I could talk to the most. Then in seventh grade our hormones switched on. And she got all…hot, and I got all stupid. And I fell in love with her. We'd stayed friends because she never knew anything about it. Because I was too much of a loser to tell her. Clearly, in this version of my life I *did* tell her somehow. I only wished I could find out how I'd done it.

"Just…" I searched my mind. There was literally no way I could explain what was happening to me. Not without her and everyone else thinking I was on drugs. "I wrote a song this morning in English class." Not sure why I said that, but what the heck.

She sipped her juice. "What else is new? What was this one about?"

"About me being stupid."

She frowned at me, shaking her head. "You're not stupid, Darren. I wish you'd stop saying that."

"Do I say it a lot?"

"Almost every day. Lots of people have problems reading. It's really no big deal."

She reached over and took my hand. I looked around to see if anyone would react. No one did. They all seemed just as used to the idea of me and Susan Koh as a thing as she was. I wondered how long it had been going on.

"So...don't we have an anniversary soon?" It was a long shot, but I was desperate.

"Of what?" Susan said.

"Uh...the...uh, first time we..."

She let go of my hand, sitting back. "What are you talking about? We started dating in February, remember? Valentine's Day year before last? And the big confession?"

"Oh, yeah." What big confession? Who had confessed? And for a year and half I'd been dating the love of my middle-grade life and I remembered nothing about it? This was going to drive me crazy. I took a breath and decided to try something else. Maybe it wouldn't give me answers, but it might make me feel better.

"Susan, would you still like me if I was rich and famous?"

She smiled back at me so brightly it made my heart hurt. "You *are* going to be rich and famous one day. And yes, I'll still like you."

So far, so good. I forged ahead. "What if I became one of those famous people who gets messed up on drugs?"

"I'd put you in rehab. But I can't see that happening. You don't even drink."

That was a surprise. In the other life, whatever it was, I was quite the party boy.

Maybe Susan had been a good influence on me.

"What if girls threw themselves all over me?"

She narrowed her eyes. "Is that what you want? Girls all over you?"

"No!" I meant it too. I didn't want a house full of drunk girls in tight dresses. I wanted Susan. I still wanted her after all these years. It almost made me feel like crying. Because I could have been with her. Even in the other life. If I hadn't screwed it up, we could have been together. It made my head hurt to think of how I'd treated her. But, of course, this Susan didn't know anything about it.

"Susan, what if I was famous and we weren't together…" I started.

"I'm not sure I like this game," she said. "Are you breaking up with me?"

"No! No way! I'm just trying to figure something out. For a song."

She looked like she didn't believe me. But after three years of dodging paparazzi questions, I was used to that.

"Okay," she said. "Go on."

"So what if I was famous, and we weren't together. Like, we'd never had the big Valentine's Day confession. And what if I hadn't seen you in over a year. And I was doing a big show and I sent you tickets and backstage passes."

She sighed happily. "I'd be pretty thrilled, I guess. That is, if I still liked you."

That should have made me happy. But it made me miserable. Because of what really happened. I just went on with it, because I thought I deserved the pain.

"What if after my show you came backstage and I was so busy being a superstar and getting wasted and letting girls crawl all over me that I... ignored you?"

She stopped smiling. "Would you do that?"

"No! Of course not. But what if I *did*? Would you ever forgive me?"

"This is going to be a depressing song, Darren. Not really your style."

"Would you, Susan? Would you forgive me if I was a jerk like that?"

She was silent for a moment. A little frown of concentration wrinkled her forehead.

"I think maybe I'd never want to talk to you again," she said.

Chapter Six

Susan hugged me before leaving me outside my history class. I stood there like an idiot, with birds twittering around my head, until someone shoved me through the door and into a seat at the back. The teacher was already talking about the electoral something. I slipped my backpack under my desk and dug out my phone again.

Maybe I had Facebook, I thought. That could have some answers. As I scrolled through the apps, a shadow fell over my desk.

I looked up to see my history teacher, a mean-looking Asian guy, frowning down at me.

"Third time this week, Darren," he said.

"I'm sorry." I shoved the phone away, zipping my backpack shut.

"You know the rule, Darren." He pointed to a poster on the wall. It was a cartoon, so I didn't have to struggle to read it. Three cell phones in a row, then an equals sign, then a picture of a sad-looking loser in the principal's office.

"See you tomorrow, kid," he said.

I groaned, gathered my stuff and walked out of there feeling like a criminal.

The hallway was deserted. I sort of remembered the way to the office, but I dreaded going there. There would be some kind of lecture about phone use and probably a whole lot of stuff about my record of rule breaking. A record I knew nothing about. It could get really awkward. I'd had enough awkward for the day. But I trudged toward the office. What choice did I have?

"Hey, D!"

I turned around. The hallway was empty. Great. I was hearing voices on top of everything else. That was perfect.

"D!"

A face poked out from the door to the stairway. It was Keir—the long-haired stoner from the bus. He seemed to know me. And he seemed pretty out of it. Maybe I could get some answers from him without raising suspicions. He held the door open and I squeezed through, letting it close behind me.

"What's up, Keir?"

"You in trouble?"

"Phone in history. Third time this week."

"That's not like you."

I scratched my head. One of the only good things about this experience was that I had my hair short again. It felt pretty good. In the other life, whatever that was, Billy favored the mop-top, natural Afro image. But worn that way, my hair was so dense I couldn't scratch my head properly even when I wanted to.

"It's not?" I said. "Maybe I'm having a bad week."

Keir smirked at me. "Wanna make it better?" He held up a little baggie of weed.

Now, obviously, as a pop sensation, I'd seen my fair share of drugs. But weed was never my thing. I remembered it turning Keir into a dolt, though, when he was hanging around me in the early days. So I wasn't surprised to see him with it now. I wasn't that tempted either, except that it meant I could leave school and any further humiliation for the day. And what did I have to lose? I'd already lost my career, my house, millions of dollars and all my fans.

"Why not?" I said. "Where are we going?"

Keir headed down the stairs to the exit. "Down to the beach," he said, opening the door to freedom. "Race you!"

We bolted out across the field and onto Maple Street. Keir got a head start. A black kid chasing a white kid through the streets of Vancouver's west side in the middle of the day was one of those things my mother used to warn me about. We turned a few heads. And by the time we got down to Kitsilano Beach, we were out of breath and laughing.

"How did you get so fast?" I asked, peeling off my hoodie.

Keir was bent over, panting. "Running from the cops."

That should have been my cue to leave. But I was operating on the extra-stupid setting that day. We found a semi-secluded spot down by the outdoor pool. It was closed for the winter, so there was no reason for anyone to come around there. Keir sat on the ground cross-legged, expertly rolled a little joint and lit it up. He took a puff and handed it to me.

I held it for a second, thinking about the day I'd thought I had yesterday. The Teen Picks Awards. The party. I'd been drunk for most of it. Had that made me any happier? No. Was getting high with Keir going to help me now? No. It was more likely to turn me into a drooling idiot.

I passed the joint back to him, feeling virtuous. "Not really in the mood today."

"Whatevs."

Keir balled my hoodie up into a pillow and lay back on the pavement, puffing and staring at the cloudy sky. I decided since he was wasted it was a good time to ask him some questions and maybe figure some stuff out.

I let out an exaggerated sigh. "Man, how long has it been since we've hung out?"

"Dunno. A month? We skipped that college talk in first week and went to Starbucks."

"Oh yeah." So I wasn't always a great student. No real surprise there. "Did we used to hang out more? Before I started going out with Susan?"

"Nah, man. Not for ages. It's cool though. I get it. I'm a bit"—he made air quotes with his fingers—"high maintenance."

He sat up and tossed the end of the joint down into the water. I actually felt sorry for him. He wasn't any different from the Keir in my other life. A messed-up kid who couldn't get his act together. Probably would never amount to anything. When he'd started to fall apart, I had just flicked him off me like a bug. That had been a dick move, I realized. Imagine if your friend was a famous celebrity and they just dumped you when you had problems.

I swore at myself under my breath.

"Same," Keir said. Then he pointed down the shore to the yacht club. "See those boats? I sleep in them some nights. When things get too hairy at my place."

I didn't know what to say about that. In my other life, Keir's mother had always been a bit flaky. His dad was long gone, but there was a boyfriend or someone. Keir hadn't liked him much. His home situation must have been pretty bad if he was sleeping in boats now.

It started to rain a little bit. Keir put my hoodie on. I was going to let him keep it, but he figured it out. In that way stoned people figure things out. Slowly.

"Sorry, dude." He took my hoodie off and handed it back to me. I put it on as he just sat there getting wet. And I felt like an even bigger douchebag than I was in my other life. Or the dream or whatever it was.

Maybe *this* was the dream. I had an idea. A dumb one, but it was born of desperation.

"Dude," I said to Keir. "Pinch me."

"What?"

"Pinch me. Like you're trying to wake me up."

I thought he'd argue, like any normal person would. But he didn't. He just reached over and pinched my arm. Hard.

"Ow!" I shoved him. It was just an instinctive reaction.

He shoved me back. I jumped on him and got him in a headlock. We were playing, but not. It was a guy thing. Sometimes you just need to fight. If people understood that in school, kids would be a lot happier. Keir tried to wriggle out of the headlock by grabbing me under my arms. And I'm super ticklish, so I screamed like a girl. Now he knew my weakness. Then we were rolling around, me holding his head, rubbing my knuckles on his skull, him with his thumbs jammed in my armpits. Both of us howling like lunatics.

I suppose I shouldn't have been surprised when we took a breather and saw two cops striding toward us. A white lady and a Sikh man. They both looked very disappointed.

Keir swore. Loud. He squirmed away from me and took off so fast into the trees that he was like a blur. I knew better than to run from police. Another thing Mom had taught me.

"What's going on here, son?" the dude in the turban said as I turned back to them.

"Nothing. We were just playing around." I mean, this was Kits Beach. I was sure this cop had seen stranger things.

"Why'd your friend run?"

Okay, I was a little scared. A black kid is always a little scared of cops. That's just how it is. So I threw Keir under the bus. I'm not proud.

"He's got drugs on him."

"Do you have drugs on you?"

"No, sir."

These two cops looked at each other like they wanted to laugh at how clueless I was. Why had I left the school? I could have been warm and napping in math class at that very moment. Instead I was cold, damp and about to be frisked.

"Can you empty your pockets, please?" the lady cop said.

I reached into the pockets of my hoodie and froze, every kind of curse imaginable resonating in my head.

Keir had stashed his bag of weed in my pocket.

Chapter Seven

I'd never been in the backseat of a police car before. Not that I remembered anyway. Maybe in this version of my life I was a hooligan. I was about to find out, as the Sikh cop ran my name through his database. The lady cop leaned down through the open door.

"So you're seventeen. Why aren't you in school?"

"I got kicked out of history class for using my phone. So I bailed."

"And your friend came with you?"

"It was his idea. He's not my friend."

"And you don't know his name?"

I'd finally managed to muster a small amount of loyalty and decided to keep Keir's name out of it. Maybe he didn't deserve it. For all I knew, he'd put the weed in my pocket on purpose. But I felt like I'd already screwed up his life once, even if it was in an alternate universe or whatever. I didn't want to do it again. I shook my head.

"He's clean," the cop in the front seat said.

The lady cop almost smiled a little. I thought I might get away with it. Maybe they would just confiscate the weed and drive me back to the school. But the cop in the turban turned around.

"Here's the thing. Yesterday someone reported a kid selling weed at the elementary school. A black kid. Know anything about that?"

My ears started to buzz again. "No. It wasn't me." But for all I knew it *could* have been me. Could I have become such a total asshat? Would I sell drugs to little kids?

"Where were you yesterday at lunchtime?"

"I don't know. I don't remember." At least that was an honest answer. I didn't know what this version of me had been doing the day before at lunch. The other version, the one I did know, had been drinking mimosas and getting a pedicure while chatting on the phone with John Legend. I started to tremble. That version of things seemed so far-fetched now. What if I *was* the black kid who was dealing drugs at the elementary school?

"You don't remember yesterday at lunch?" The lady cop sounded dubious.

I thought maybe here was a way I could get out of this. By admitting how crazy I was.

"I don't remember yesterday at all," I said, my voice shaking. "I thought I was somewhere else. But now I'm here. I don't know how I got here."

The two cops exchanged another look. "Anything on his mental history?" the lady cop said. The other dude went back to his laptop, clicking a few keys.

"Where did you think you were?" the lady said.

I closed my eyes. It was all slipping away from me. Because, of course, it must have been some kind of dream.

"I thought I was in LA," I said. And I guess the fact that I had tears in my eyes kept her from outright laughing at me. "I was getting ready to host the Teen Picks Awards."

"That Harry Potter kid hosted the Teen Picks," she told me gently. "I watched it with my sons."

Not how I remembered it. *I* was the host. Harry Potter kid presented the Best Onscreen Kiss award. I remembered it so *clearly*. How could that have been a dream?

Next thing I knew, I was sobbing. I'd never see Billy again. Or my dad. Or even Jo-Dee Justice. Why hadn't I said something to Mom as soon as I woke up? She was a nurse. She would have known what to do. My face was buried in my hands, but I felt the lady cop climb into the backseat beside me. She closed the door, reaching around me to do up my seat belt.

"You really don't remember yesterday?" she asked.

I shook my head again. "I don't remember years. I thought I was a different person. A famous singer."

She narrowed her eyes at me. "You're not making this up so we won't bust you?"

"No! I was Darius Zaire. A big star. I don't remember anything about high school. I had a house on Delfern Drive in Bel Air. And today I'm going out with Susan Koh, but I thought I was dating Jo-Dee Justice."

The cop in the front seat snorted. "Jo-Dee Justice bats for the other team, kid. Everyone knows that. She's dating the girl from that Netflix show."

The lady cop shushed him, putting her hand on my knee. I was trembling so bad I made her shake too.

"Did you hit your head when you were fighting with your friend?"

"I don't think so."

"What about weird pills or mushrooms? Have you taken anything like that? Or smoked anything?"

"I don't know. I don't think so."

Leaning back, she held my face and looked into my eyes. Then she shrugged at her partner. He started the car.

"We're going to take you to the ER, okay?" the lady said. "They can check you out, and we'll call your mom."

"What about the drugs?"

"Don't worry about that for now. Let's get this figured out."

I stared out the window all the way to the hospital. Before my career took off, I lived on the other side of the town, so these streets weren't that familiar to me. But surely if this was my real life I should recognize something. I'd apparently been going to school on this side for years. But nothing rang a bell until we got onto Broadway. I remembered the bookstore. And a sushi joint Mom and I liked.

At the hospital, the cops hung around until a doctor came to see me. But before he could even get two words out, Mom arrived.

"Darren! Oh, Darren, baby, what happened?"

She threw her arms around me and started asking the doctor all kinds of medical questions. What was my blood pressure, my pulse? Had they taken blood? How were my pupils?

When she calmed down a bit, a nurse took her away to fill out a few forms, and the doctor was able to talk to me.

"It says here you have memory loss."

"Yeah. I guess." It wasn't that I'd lost memories, but that I had the wrong memories. How was I going to explain that?

"What's the last thing you remember?"

"All I can remember is today. I mean…it's hard to explain."

He shone a light in my eyes. "Try. Just take your time."

I took a deep breath. I had to tell someone. I still had a fleeting hope in my heart that this was a prank put together by Billy. So maybe this doctor was an actor, and this was all being filmed. But they would have had hours of footage by now. Was this going to be a whole series?

It was hopeless. Obviously, I'd just lost my mind. I needed to tell the doctor everything.

"Okay. So I remember yesterday," I started. "And the day before that, and all the years back to when I was a kid. But they're the wrong memories."

"How are they wrong?" He sat on a stool with his clipboard on his lap.

"Like, I had a different life. I remember being famous. A successful musician and TV star. I had a house in LA and a manager called Billy."

He wrote something down and looked back up at me. "You're sure this wasn't just a fantasy?"

"Well, no. I'm not sure. But if it was a fantasy, then why can't I remember anything else? My real life? I go to a normal school and I have a girlfriend and I don't remember any of it."

"Nothing?"

"No. I didn't know any of my teachers' names. I didn't even know what classes I have. I don't remember how my girlfriend and I got together."

"But you remember her?"

"Yes! Yes, I remember her, but only because we were friends before I became a star."

The doctor frowned at me. I was sure he'd never heard anything so ridiculous. But I also hoped that this was some known syndrome caused by chemical additives or radiation or something.

"Have you taken any narcotics recently, Darren?" he asked.

"I don't know. I don't remember. Not in the other life. I was a little drunk last night, but no drugs."

"Do you drink a lot?"

"I don't know. In the other life, once in a while. Not every day. I'm working too hard."

"Have you hit your head recently? Playing sports or in a car accident?"

"I don't know. Wait! I fell out of bed this morning."

"How high is your bed? Is it a bunk bed?"

"No. Just a normal bed. I landed on LEGO."

I was pretty sure he wrote down the word *LEGO*. Then he stood up. "I'm going to order a few tests. We'll test your blood for drugs. Is there going to be a big freak-out with your mom if that comes up positive?"

"Maybe. Probably. But I don't care. I'll go to rehab if I need to. I want to get better. This is really messing me up." I had to clench my fists to keep from crying again.

"Okay. It might not be that. So we're going to refer you for a CAT scan and an EEG on your brain. See what's going on there. And I'm going to get a psychiatrist to talk to you."

That sounded bad. "Am I going crazy?"

Maybe he was trying to look reassuring, but he just looked grim. He wasn't filling me with confidence. "Let's wait to see what the tests tell us," he said.

Chapter Eight

The psychiatrist was not on duty, so we
made an appointment for the next day.
The other tests all came up negative. No
brain tumor or stroke. Normal brain-
waves. No drugs apart from a tiny bit of
alcohol. I thought that was weird, since
Susan had said I didn't drink. But I
didn't have time to think about what that

meant because Mom was busy lecturing me as we drove home.

"You were playing that ridiculous video game all last night. Were you drinking in your room?"

"I don't know, Mom. I don't remember. Remember? In the other life I was at a party. At my house."

"Drinking?"

"Yes, I was drinking. It was a party."

"What have I told you about drinking, Darren? Do you want to end up like your father?"

"It might have only been a dream, Mom! Don't get all mad at me over something I dreamed."

She drove in silence for a few minutes. Then something she said finally clicked.

"Wait. What happened to Dad?" I asked.

We were at a red light. She stopped and looked at me. I did not like the expression on her face. She turned back to the road before answering. "Your father is in jail. He was driving drunk and he nearly killed someone." It was two red lights later before she spoke again. "You really don't remember that? We went to the trial."

In my other life Dad was kind of a loser, but he hadn't relapsed into drinking until he started hanging around me again. And then I'd just shunted him in and out of rehab. He never drove. And he never hurt anyone. So maybe he was just going to start drinking again anyway. Maybe that wasn't my fault. Maybe my keeping an eye on him had kept him out of serious trouble.

"I…in the dream he was there. At the party. And I was going to send him to rehab. There was no trial."

We pulled into the driveway of the townhouse. Mom parked and turned to me again. "Maybe this is some kind of coping thing for you. It's been kind of tough these last few years. The thing with your dad and the dyslexia and the new school. Maybe you just made up this better version of your life and for some reason it started feeling real."

I looked up as our front door opened. Susan was standing there, outlined by the hall light.

"I'm not sure which version is better, Mom. I hardly ever see you in the other life. And I'm not with Susan."

Mom smiled. "And the millions of dollars didn't make up for that?"

"Not really," I said. And in that moment, I meant it.

"I came as soon as you called," Susan said to my mom as we got out of the car. "There's a pizza in the oven, and I made a salad."

Mom gave her a little kiss on the cheek. "You're a treasure," she said as we went inside. Susan seemed pretty friendly with my mom, and as she finished setting the table I could see she was familiar with our house. It was weird, like we were married or something. In Darius's life, the girl-friends, such as they were, never left LA, so Mom never met any of them.

I blinked as I realized I was starting to think of Darius as another person.

Susan and I sat at the table, waiting for the pizza to be done.

"Your mom says you lost your memory," Susan said.

"Something like that."

"She said you've been having some kind of delusions."

"I guess so."

She looked at me, taking my hand. I felt like falling into her eyes. "And you don't remember us being together?"

"No," I confessed. "I'm sorry."

"Your mom says the delusions are about being a famous pop star. Plain old

Susan Koh, band nerd, is probably not that exciting in comparison."

I wanted to put my arms around her. I remembered all those times I had wanted to do that when we were younger, before the fame and everything. I had never had the guts then. I still didn't. I just sat there like an idiot. Finally I gathered my wits enough to speak.

"Honestly?" I said, taking her other hand. "This life seems like a dream come true."

She looked a bit taken aback and was about to say something else when the oven beeped.

"I'll get it!" Mom called from the other room.

Susan and Mom put the dinner on the table. I wasn't feeling very hungry, but I ate two pieces of pizza and a bit of salad just to be polite. After dinner Mom disappeared into the office nook while Susan and I talked some more.

"Can you tell me about us?" I asked her. "Maybe it will shake some memories loose. Like, what was the big Valentine's Day confession?"

Susan blushed a little, looking down at her empty plate. "It was really sweet," she said. "This other boy, Brian Merk—remember him?"

I shook my head.

"Well, anyway. He put on this big performance, made a whole ridiculous day out of trying to ask me out. There were flowers and chocolates and balloons, and it was utterly mortifying."

I sat there hoping whatever I'd done was equally impressive. I couldn't imagine it. Darius had never been much good at making advances. Usually, he just let girls fall into his lap.

"What did I do?" I asked.

"Nothing," Susan said. "At the end of the day, you were helping me carry all this crap Brian had given me home and I asked you if you thought I should go out with him. You said no. Because you thought I should go out with *you*."

She smiled, lost in the memory.

"That's it?" I asked. "That was the great Valentine's Day confession?"

"Yep. You don't remember it, huh?"

I shook my head again.

"So in this other life," Susan started gently. "Are you seeing anyone? Do you have a girlfriend?"

I opened my mouth to answer, because I thought the story about me dating a lesbian pop singer would probably make Susan laugh. I wanted to see her laugh. But Mom interrupted.

"Darren!" she called out from the office. "Don't forget the dishes."

"Mom! I'm having a mental breakdown. Can't I get a break?"

Susan laughed behind her hand. It was always so cute when she did that.

My mom appeared in the doorway. "The doctor said keeping to a normal routine might help. Dishes are normal. Get to it."

Susan helped me gather the plates and things and take them into the kitchen. I looked around. It was the same house I'd grown up in, but the kitchen looked a bit different. I opened the dishwasher, inspecting it.

"Let me guess," Susan said. "You've forgotten how to use a dishwasher?"

I just shrugged helplessly.

"You rinse, I'll load," she said.

Chapter Nine

After much negotiation, Mom agreed to let me walk Susan home. I was sure she would watch the entire journey on the helicopter-parent surveillance app on her phone. And anyway, it was only two blocks. In Vancouver. What could happen?

We held hands while I tried to squeeze any kind of memory out of my brain.

I wasn't sure how to act with her. I mean, how close were we? How serious? How did we normally act around each other? I didn't even know how to talk to her anymore. When we were friends as kids, we used to make each other laugh until we cried by saying stupid things. After walking for a few minutes in silence, I decided to try that.

"Isn't it gross how elephants drink by sucking water into their noses and squirting it into their mouths? Imagine if we drank that way."

She laughed so explosively she nearly tripped. She was wiping tears from her eyes by the time she calmed down.

"Well, you haven't changed much," she said.

"I haven't? I'm normally funny?"

"Darren, you're so funny my face hurts from smiling around you."

That made me feel better than I had all day. Even though it didn't feel very familiar. Darius put on a party persona, but really, mostly if he—if *I* wasn't performing, I just wanted to play my piano and be alone. I thought about the song I'd performed in English class.

"Do I write songs a lot? Like the one I did in English class today?"

She tugged me around a corner. I remembered where she lived, and this wasn't the way. Maybe they had moved.

"You write songs all the time," she said.

"Have I ever written a song for you?"

She went quiet for a moment, as the lyrics and tune to my first big hit, "Something to Tell You," rattled through my head.

"Not really," she said. "There was this funny song you wrote last year. It was about girls and their inappropriate winter shoes. Apparently, I inspired that one."

I pulled her to a stop. I knew the song she was talking about. Billy had wanted me to have a Christmas hit, so I'd written this stupid thing about girls slipping on the ice.

"'Catch You at Christmas'? That one?" I said.

"Yes!" She clutched my hands excitedly. "You remember that?"

I nodded down at her. But I didn't want to tell her that in my version, the song had been inspired by a bunch of fangirls who had followed me around at the Sundance Film Festival. I thought again of the song from English class, how I had known the lyrics somehow. It seemed like music was the thing the different versions of my life had in common. Maybe that meant something.

We stared at each other. God. She was so pretty.

"Well," she said, pointing across the street. "That's my house."

I studied the two-story cottage, trying to remember it. "You lived in a duplex before, didn't you?"

"Yeah, but we moved in ninth grade." She pulled me across the road. "You've lost everything that far back, huh?"

"Most things, it seems. I wish I could remember, you know, us. It's weird not knowing how we are together."

We stopped at the bottom of her front stairs. "What do you want to know about us?" she asked.

I looked down at her face, which was lit up by the streetlamp and her front porch light. "Well, I mean, do we…like…kiss and everything?"

She smiled shyly. "We kiss. But no everything. We want to wait."

"Oh. Okay." I couldn't move. I was literally paralyzed at the idea of kissing her. Nothing happened for so long that it got awkward.

"What about in your other life?" Susan asked, breaking the silence. "Do you…do *everything*?"

Oh crap, I thought. Did I have to tell her what a dirtbag I was? I thought about lying, but what was the point in lying about what was probably a delusion? That seemed doubly crazy.

"I mean, I'm pretty famous, so… yeah. You know…there's…"

"Groupies?"

She made it sound even more douchey than it was. And worse, if it *was* just a delusion, what kind of sad pervert would have a delusion like that? My head was starting to spin. I looked up at her house, wishing I could just start this day over with my brain working properly.

"I should go in," Susan said. "I have a lab report to write." She put her arms around my waist, turning her face up to me. "I can't believe you don't remember kissing me." She stood up on her toes and kissed me.

I didn't see stars. I didn't see anything. I closed my eyes and felt like I was falling into a black hole. No sound. No light. Nothing but Susan's sweet little lips on mine.

It was over too soon. I kept my eyes closed for a second. Maybe when I opened them things would be different. We'd be outside my house in LA. I didn't worry about the logic of Susan coming back with me to my other life. I kept my arms around her though, just in case.

When I opened my eyes we were still standing at the bottom of her stairs, nose to nose.

"Don't look so disappointed," she said.

"I'm not! I don't…what?"

"To you, wasn't that the first time we've ever kissed? And this is the face you make?" She demonstrated—

a pouty, perplexed face. I could see how that might feel a bit insulting.

"I'm sorry. I just…thought that might break the spell."

"The spell? You mean the curse of being a normal guy with a nerdy Asian girlfriend?"

"That's not what I meant."

She wriggled out of my arms. I didn't know whether I should just tell her that I loved her. Had we exchanged the L word yet? I didn't want to drop it on her for the first time in such a messed-up situation.

"I know you're not yourself tonight, Darren. Don't worry about it."

I took a step back, out of her personal space. It felt upsettingly final. Like we'd just broken up. I wanted to say something to make that feeling go away, but I couldn't think of anything.

Instead she kissed me on the cheek. "Be careful walking home," she said. "Don't get lost. I'll see you tomorrow."

Then, before I could say anything more, she turned and ran up the stairs and through her front door.

When I got back to my house, Keir Brewster was sitting on my front step.

"You asshole," I said.

"Dude, I'm so sorry. It was a total accident."

I felt like I should punch his stupid face, but that would have probably just made things worse. I sat next to him on the step.

"You're lucky I didn't give them your name. I probably would have, but…" How could I explain to him what had happened? That I'd started raving about another life?

"I heard you ended up in the ER," he said.

"Jesus," I said. Apparently normal high school kids had no more privacy than pop superstars. "I think I'm having some kind of breakdown. I've got amnesia or something. The doctors don't know what's causing it."

"I thought there must have been something going on."

"You did? Why?" I didn't remember Keir as being very intuitive.

"Dude, you smiled at me on the bus."

"So?"

"So you hate me. Last time I tried to talk to you, you said, *Get away from me, you freak*."

"Didn't we go to Starbucks last month, like you said?"

"That was with about ten other people."

A giant semitruck barreled past, rattling me to the core. Or maybe I was just rattled. It didn't help that I didn't know why I hated Keir. He seemed all right.

"So I don't hang out with you normally?" I asked.

"No, not for ages."

"And I don't do drugs?"

"Nope. You're clean as a Mormon. Susan's not into that, so…" He made a whipping noise, flicking his hand back and forth.

"So why did you offer me drugs at school?"

"Dunno. You seemed a bit tense. I was just being friendly. I guess." It was a bit sad that that was his idea of friendly.

I shook my head. "The cops said some black kid has been dealing drugs at the little kids' school. They thought it was me."

"Ha! You? Not likely. Anyway, I know that guy. He's older. And a lowlife."

That was a relief. Of all the possibilities in this unknown life, the idea that I'd lost enough morals to sell drugs to kids was the most worrying. I still didn't know who I was, but at least I wasn't a lowlife.

Keir pulled out a pack of cigarettes and was about to light one.

"No way, man," I said. "My mom will flip her lid."

He chuckled as he tucked the smokes away. "Fine, whatever," he said. "Why don't you tell me about this amnesia?"

So I did. I told him everything. About falling asleep in my mansion with a skinny white girl crawling all over me, about her pushing me off the leather couch, about waking up as I hit the floor in my old room. And about not remembering anything that went with this version of my life. That was key. If the other life was a delusion, surely I would remember a few things about my *real* life. But I didn't. It was all gone.

"Do you think Darren Zegers from this world is currently in Darius Zaire's world, hooking up with the skinny white girl?" Keir asked.

"God, I hope not," I said. "She was a skank." Then I processed what he'd said. "Wait a minute. You believe me? You think this is real?"

"I don't know. Maybe. Like some kind of quantum wormhole thing. Or aliens! Maybe you're being tested."

That made me laugh. If this was a test, I was pretty sure I was failing.

Chapter Ten

Mom scowled at Keir when I brought him inside. Mom was not a scowler most of the time. At least, when I was a kid, in the life that I remembered, she had been one of those moms who stuffs your friends with homemade cookies. But she didn't seem to like Keir.

"What's the deal with us?" I asked him when we got up to my room.

"What do you mean?"

"You said I hate you. My mom clearly doesn't like you, and she likes everyone. Is there some kind of history I should know about?"

Keir plopped down onto my bed, kicking a music magazine out of the way. He fluffed up my pillow and lay down like he owned the place.

"We were pals when we were little. You remember that?" he asked.

"Yeah." In my version of history, in the Darius Zaire version, Keir had come out to Toronto with me as kind of a paid bestie on the TV-show set. But he'd fallen in with some creepy stoners in the crew. Then, when he'd come on tour with me, he'd started using drugs big-time, and his mom, who had been doing my hair and makeup, had taken him home. I never really knew what happened to him after that. That is, Darius never knew.

Nor cared, I realized. That was a dick move too.

"Well anyway, now I'm kind of a stoner and you aren't down with that, so..." He shrugged. "It's probably my fault. I can get a little...much. Sometimes, when I'm wasted."

I looked at him properly for the first time that day. He was pale and skinny, with dark circles under his eyes. "Maybe you should cool it with the drugs for a while, Keir. We can start hanging out again, if you want."

"You don't need my kind of trouble in your life, bro. You've got to figure out your own problems first."

That was certainly true. "I've got an appointment with a shrink tomorrow," I said.

Keir rolled his eyes. "Shrinks. What do they know? What questions can he ask you that you can't ask yourself?"

He had a point. I had barely had a moment since I'd got up to really think about it. Maybe I could figure it out by myself if I just took some time to stop panicking.

"What kind of questions?" I asked.

Keir sat up, leaning on the wall with his legs crossed. "Well, start with…is there anything from this life that seems familiar?"

I searched my brain, running the events of the day over in my head. Then I remembered English class. "Music!" I said. "This morning I made up a song in English class. I thought I just freestyled it, but then I found the lyrics written in my notebook. I must have—I mean, this version of me must have written them."

"Okay. Good start."

"And then Susan told me that I made up a funny song for her. About wearing the wrong shoes in the snow.

And that song is in the other life too. It's one of my biggest hits. Darius's biggest hits, I mean."

Keir nodded, a thoughtful expression on his face. "It makes sense."

"It does? What does?"

"Well, music is your life. You're obsessed with it. So it makes sense that music would be the crossover point."

Crossover point. He made it sound so plausible, as though there was something scientific about it. "What do you think it means?"

He shrugged. "Where did this other life start? It must have been a song, right? Your first hit?"

"Yes!" I thought for a second. "Maybe if I play it...something will happen. I'll go back, or I'll remember my real life. Or something."

We were making it up as we went along, based on nothing but me being desperate and Keir being stoned and philosophical. But it was worth a shot. Once again, what did I have to lose?

I pulled my guitar out from behind my overflowing hamper. After tuning it up I started playing my song, the song that had made me a star: "Something to Tell You." Keir just sat there listening, a sort of dazed expression on his face. I finished the song and looked around. Nothing seemed to have changed. My room was the same. The house was the same. I could hear Mom rattling around in the kitchen. I reached up to feel my hair. Still the short fade. No mop-top in sight. So much for my theory.

"I've heard that song before," Keir said.

"You have? Not on the radio, I hope." That would be just my luck. Some other loser making bank off *my* song.

"No. You wrote it years ago," Keir said. "Like, when we were twelve.

You were going to play it for Susan, but you chickened out."

That was weird. If I wrote the song, why hadn't I played it for Susan? Especially now that we were going out. It was a pretty romantic song. And girls love that kind of stuff. It seemed strange that Susan didn't know about it. Maybe I'd forgot about it in the years between when I wrote it and when Susan and I started going together. Or maybe…

"Holy crap," I said.

"What?"

"What if *that song* is the crossover point? Because that's where the two lives split apart. In one life I record the song and put it on YouTube and become a star. In the other I never play it again. Maybe the song crossed over into the other life. That's why I never played it again in this life."

"Like you forgot it?" Keir asked.

"I must have! Why else wouldn't Susan know about it? I would have told her. Played it for her. Did I ever play it again that you know of?"

"No, you just played it that one time. You wanted to know what I thought of it." Keir rubbed his face. "This is so weird, man."

I just nodded. I'd never been into science or science fiction and all that *Star Trek*-type stuff. I was starting to wish I'd paid a bit more attention to it.

"It's clear what you have to do though," Keir said.

"It is?" It wasn't clear to me. Nothing was clear to me. Not even my own name.

But Keir seemed pretty confident. He put his hand on my shoulder, talking to me like he was some kind of wise mentor. "You have to play the song for Susan," he said.

Chapter Eleven

"I feel like an idiot," I said. And I was cold. Keir had made me change into nicer clothes—good dress pants and a shirt. But I didn't have a blazer, so now I was freezing.

"You *look* like an idiot," Keir said.

"I don't even know which one is Susan's window."

We looked up at the dark cottage. Susan had said she had homework, so maybe she'd still be up. It wasn't that late.

"This is a dumb idea," I said.

"It's the only idea I have," Keir said. "Do you have a better one?"

I didn't. And if I was honest with myself, I kind of liked the idea of serenading Susan. It would be a perfectly weird way to end the weirdest day of my two lives.

"It's probably that one," Keir said, pointing down the side of the house. "My cousins live in a house just like this, and the smaller bedroom is there."

We walked down the side of the house, trying not to trip in the dark. The light was on in the room, but the curtain was drawn, so we couldn't see in. I had some doubts, but they were outweighed by Keir massaging my shoulders like a coach before a boxing match.

"You can do this," he said.

It sounded familiar. I felt as though he'd told me that before. I shook my head to clear it, then played the first chords of the song.

"*You're the one who knows me best*," I sang. "*The one who listens when I talk too much…*"

I was pretty shaky, but as I played on, I started to feel more like confident Darius Zaire and less like dweeby Darren Zegers. By the time the curtain twitched aside, I was in the chorus, hitting the high emotive notes like a pro. Susan's face appeared in the window. She looked more astonished than impressed, but I'd take it.

"*I've got something to tell you*," I sang. "*And it can't wait a minute more…*"

"It bloody well can wait a minute!" someone shouted from the house next door. "Some of us are trying to watch *The Daily Show.*"

I stopped singing. Susan just shook her head and gestured to the back of her house.

"It was Keir's idea," I said when she opened the back door. Keir, I noticed, was nowhere to be seen. Some friend. That was twice in one day he'd bailed on me when things got tense.

"Since when do you hang around with Keir?" Susan asked. She stepped aside and let me in. I followed her into the living room.

"What happened there anyway? With Keir? Didn't we used to be friends?"

"He was okay when we were younger, but he started getting wasted all the time, and now he's just a bore."

I sat next to her on the couch. It seemed pretty harsh to unfriend someone just because they were a bore. I wondered if there was something more to it.

"Did you just write that song?" Susan said, changing the subject back to what it was supposed to be.

"No...I..." I didn't even want to say it. It sounded so dumb.

"It's from the other life?" Susan supplied helpfully.

"Yeah."

"So you didn't write it just for me?"

"No! I did. Only I was too scared to sing it to you, so I made a video and put it on YouTube. It went viral before I could even tell you."

"And that was that? You took off and got famous and forgot about me?"

I held her hands. "I never forgot about you, Susan. I tried to see you again, but I screwed it up."

She sat back, studying me for a moment. "So you really *did* ignore me backstage at one of your shows? Like you said at school today?"

"I'm sorry. I never forgave myself for that. I was a bit of a mess in the early days. After that I..." I zoned out for a second, remembering everything. *Keir* had been there that night. We'd got really drunk together. And I'd been so mad at him the next day. I'd blamed him. So I'd kicked him out of my life.

What. An. Asshole.

"After that you what?" Susan asked.

I sighed. "I cleaned up my act a bit." But I hadn't. All I'd done was get rid of a few bad influences who got me into trouble. Like Keir.

"Sounds like you weren't such a bad person in this other life," Susan said. "Do you want to go back?"

I wasn't sure anymore. I wasn't sure if it was even real. And even if it was real, did I really want to go back? I'd been miserable most of the time.

A drunk dad. A fake girlfriend. A manager who never listened to me.

"It was nice that I could buy my mom a condo," I said. "And a car. I bought her a Prius. And I saw a lot more of my dad and tried to help him out, too, with his addiction. So he wasn't in jail, at least."

Susan just nodded. She really was the only person who knew how to listen to me. She was also listening as though I wasn't crazy, which meant a lot.

"But I would miss you, Susan," I said. "I *did* miss you." And I finally gathered enough courage to kiss her. This time it lasted a little longer and went a little further. My head was spinning by the time we pulled apart. "I wish I had sung the song for you when I wrote it. Then maybe everything would be different."

"Everything *is* different," she reminded me.

I wanted to believe that. But I didn't know how long I could go on not knowing who I was.

"You don't look convinced," Susan said.

"What if I never get over this? Or if it's because I have a brain tumor or something?"

"I don't think it's a brain tumor. It could be something as simple as a virus," Susan offered.

I had been one of those kids who rarely got sick. Trust me to go all out with my first time. Amnesia and delusions. If this was a virus, it was the Rolls Royce of viruses.

"I remember I had the flu once," Susan said, pulling my head down to her shoulder. "I felt so sick I was sure I was never going to get better."

I knew that feeling well. Hangovers feel like that.

"But then I went to sleep one night, and in the morning I was better. Maybe it'll be like that."

She was right. About the flu *and* hangovers. Things always look much better after a decent night's sleep.

"You're right. I should just go home and go to bed."

Susan pouted a little—the cutest thing ever. "It's not that late. Why don't you watch *Doctor Who* with me and then go home?"

That sounded awesome. We snuggled up, and I tucked a blanket around us as Susan logged into Netflix and chose an episode.

I was asleep before the first alien even appeared.

Chapter Twelve

I woke up in a puddle of spit. "Susan?" I mumbled as I rolled over, taking a deep breath. I smelled stale beer, strawberries and leather.

Leather?

"SUSAN!" I yelled, sitting bolt upright.

But she wasn't there with me under the cozy blanket in her living room.

Because I wasn't there either. I was in my games room, sticking to my leather couch. I wiped my hands over my face and head. Smooth shave and shaggy afro. I shook my head, staring around the room in a daze.

"What a weird dream," I said to no one. I sat there, stretching and waking up, thinking about Susan and how good it had felt to be with her. How normal and healthy. And *real*. The dream had felt very real. I looked around, half expecting this reality to dissolve again, to change back to Susan's house in Vancouver. But it didn't.

The room was just how I had left it at the end of the party. Empty beer bottles and chip bowls on the Noguchi coffee table. Game controllers strewn around. Trixie with two *e*'s was nowhere to be seen. Thank God. I looked at my giant screen TV as though I wasn't sure what its purpose was. Why would I want such a big TV?

I could hear the vacuum running downstairs. So Gloria had arrived and was dealing with whatever toxic mess the party had left all over my house. All the hangers-on would have slithered away by now. I hoped so anyway.

I struggled to my feet, surprised that I didn't seem to have a hangover. In fact, I felt more well rested than I had in months. Settled almost, with none of that churning feeling in my brain. My thoughts felt orderly and sensible for once. I stood up and pulled my jeans on before padding barefoot out into the hall.

In the room next to the games room, I found my dad, tucked into bed like a little kid. I nudged him awake. He opened one bloodshot eye, glaring at me.

"Hey," I said. "You're going to rehab today."

"Urgh."

"I'm going to set up some therapy for us when you get out, so we can sort out our issues."

He opened his other eye, suddenly alert. "What issues?" he asked.

"Issues, Dad. We have multiple issues. We need to deal with them before something bad happens. Go back to sleep."

He frowned cluelessly at me for a second before pulling the blankets over his head and rolling over.

In my office, I found Billy doing whatever it was he did on my computer. Counting my money probably.

"Billy!" I said. "I'm getting a haircut, and you can't stop me." I left before he even got a word out.

Downstairs, Gloria scowled at me, flicking the vacuum off halfway through addressing some kind of popcorn-related incident on my faux-zebra rug.

"Do I pay you enough?" I asked.

"No," she said.

"If you tell me where my phone is, I'll double it."

That made her smile a bit. Deep down, Gloria loved me. "Charging in the kitchen."

It was right where she said, with a full battery. I unplugged it and flicked it on, not sure if I had the guts to do what I had in mind. I still remembered Susan's phone number. Maybe it had changed though. Maybe I should Facebook her first. Or maybe a text. Yes. A text. That was safe. I punched in her number and typed out a text.

This is Darius/Darren. Just wanted to say hi.

Friendly. Not creepy. No spelling mistakes either. Not bad for a dyslexic. I sent it, feeling pretty smug.

Gloria had made coffee. As I was digging a coffee cup out of the dishwasher, my phone rang. I snatched it up and checked the number.

It was Susan calling back. I nearly dropped the phone in the sink. Then I panicked for a half a second. Then I gave myself a stern talking-to and clicked *Answer*.

"Hello?"

"Darren? Is he there? Is he with you?"

"What?" She sounded upset. Frantic even. "Is who here?" I asked.

"Keir! Is Keir with you?"

What was going on? Was this some kind of hybrid world between whatever that weird dream was and my real life? "I haven't seen Keir in years," I said. "Why? What's wrong?"

Suddenly I could hear that she was crying. Her voice broke as she explained it to me. "We had a big fight. He's been really unwell. He hasn't been taking his medications, and he's…" She stopped, sobbing into the phone. "He was drinking again, I think!" she cried. "I thought he might have crossed the border somehow and been on the way down to LA to see you. He left his phone at home. He's been missing for two days!"

I stared into the dishwasher while I processed what she'd said. And a horrible realization dawned on me. "Susan, are you and Keir a couple now?"

She sniffed and blew her nose. "He's changed, Darren," she said. "He was doing so much better and finally getting proper treatment for his anxiety. And he's really so sweet. But the pressure of starting twelfth grade was getting to him. And his stepdad was being a real bastard. I tried to be there for him, but..." She cried some more while I listened. Listened to my heart breaking into little tiny pieces.

Keir and Susan. I never would have predicted it. But life was strange.

I guessed my dream was just that. A dream. I sighed and looked out at my pool. Someone had left a floaty in there. It was shaped like a little boat.

I got a sudden chill. My body shivered as goose bumps sprung up all over me.

"Holy crap, Susan! I think I know where he is!"

"What? Where?"

How could I explain it to her? That Keir had spoken to me in a dream? I made something up. Something a bit more plausible.

"You know the yacht club down by Kitsilano pool? Years ago Keir told me that he snuck into the boats there sometimes. Like when he wanted some time alone to chill."

"God, really? He never mentioned that to me. The club by Kits pool? You're sure?"

"Definitely. He pointed it out once when we were down there."

Thankfully, she didn't ask any more questions. "I've got to go. I'll call the police right now."

She hung up. And that was that.

I set the phone down and poured myself a cup of coffee. Then I sat at the kitchen table, just sipping and thinking about Susan and Keir. I hoped they found him. I hoped he was okay. All the dismissive things I'd said to him back then streamed through my head. If he was alive, I was definitely going to call and apologize. Maybe try to think of some way to make it up to him.

Billy appeared in the doorway a few minutes later.

"What's this about a haircut?"

"I'm a grown man, Billy. I can choose my own haircut." I got up and pulled another cup out of the dishwasher, pouring him some coffee. "And let's call it a day on the Jo-Dee Justice thing, okay? That's completely moronic."

He just stared at me as though he'd never met me before. But I could see that he was a little amused to see me assert myself for once. "Whatever you say, kid."

My phone beeped its text tone. I grabbed it from the table and read the message.

They found him in a boat. Cold and really sick, but alive. They think he'll be OK. Thank you SO MUCH.

Barely ten minutes had gone by. Those Vancouver cops were *fast*. But I guessed they didn't have much else to do at eleven o'clock on a Sunday morning. That made me think about how peaceful Vancouver was. And how genuine the people were. The last time I'd been there, a bunch of kids had jammed with me in the guitar store like it was no big deal. And Mom and I had eaten at our favorite sushi joint on Broadway without anyone bothering us.

"Billy," I asked, "do I have enough money to buy a nice house in Vancouver?"

"Kid, you could buy the Trans-Canada Highway and have change left over for a spaceship."

"Let's fly up there tonight. We can look at houses tomorrow. I've got to get out of LA for a while."

He frowned at me. "What's going on, buddy?" For all his controlling and superficiality, Billy really cared about me. He was like a big brother. "Are you okay? What was that text?"

"Remember Keir?" I said. Billy knew Keir. He had been with me from pretty much the start too. "I think I might have just saved his life." I told him what had just happened. "His home life is a mess. Maybe he could live with me again. We could both clean ourselves up a bit."

"Are you sure that's what you want?"

I set my coffee cup down and did the responsible thing of thinking about it for a few seconds. But it was an easy decision. It felt like the best decision I had ever made.

"It is. I had a…" I stopped. Should I tell him about the dream or vision or out-of-body experience or whatever it was? He would probably think I'd lost my mind. "An epiphany," I finally said. I'd always loved that word. I loved the idea of understanding something suddenly in a bright flash of light.

"Epiphanies are good," Billy said with a grin. "Let me go call the airline. See if I can hire a private jet. That's always fun."

He disappeared back upstairs. Billy was pretty easygoing when it came down to it. And he was as efficient as hell. I knew he'd work out a way of checking my dad into rehab, doubling Gloria's pay and breaking up with Jo-Dee before we got on the plane. The idea of the private jet reminded me of something.

I yelled up the stairs, "Oh, and Billy? I'm giving up drinking! No cocktails on the plane!"

"You're breaking my heart, kid!" he yelled back down.

What are a couple of broken hearts between old friends? I finished my coffee and headed out into the living room, where the piano was. I wanted to write a song. Something meaningful for a change. I'd been planning for my next album to be different. More mature. It was time for me to evolve into a real artist instead of a cheesy pop idol. This song could be the start.

I thought I might call it "Crossover Point."

Acknowledgements

First shout-out goes to Orca Book Publishers for creating and promoting the Soundings imprint, as well as their other lines for "undiscovered" readers. It's always so fun to meet librarians and teachers from around the world who are familiar with Orca's books and depend on them for use with kids.

Thanks to Andrew Wooldridge for having faith that I could make this rather strange little story work and to Tanya Trafford for doing such a good job editing it.

Many people helped me get the details of this book right. Thanks go to Hannah Gomèz and Brent Lambert for helping with cultural aspects of my biracial protagonist and Max Livant for helping with musical terms and 21st century slang—always a challenge!

Thanks also to my daughter Lucy, for being a live-in youth consultant.

Of course the rest of my family, my long suffering husband, my sisters and mom also deserve thanks for their unflagging support.

Finally to all you "undiscovered" readers out there—you give what I do special meaning. Thanks!

Gabrielle Prendergast has written several books for young people, including *Audacious, Capricious* and *Pandas on the Eastside*. She lives in Vancouver, British Columbia, with her husband, daughter and varying numbers of chickens. For more information, visit www.angelhorn.com.

Titles in the Series

orca soundings

orca soundings

For more information on all the books
in the Orca Soundings series, please visit
www.orcabook.com.